# NO FISH FOR CHARLES

BY TRACY DETZ

ILLUSTRATED BY MONIKA SUSKA

ISBN: 978-1-7338973-1-0 (hard cover)
ISBN: 978-1-7338973-2-7 (soft cover)

Edited by: Amy Ashby

Published by Warren Publishing
Charlotte, NC
www.warrenpublishing.net
Printed in the United States

FOR **RYDER,** MY IMAGINATIVE DREAMER
AND **TRYSTAN,** MY FREE SPIRIT.

My name is Charles
and I'm a big croc!
I love to chill on top of a rock.
But, my favorite thing I like to do
is fish from the back of my big canoe.

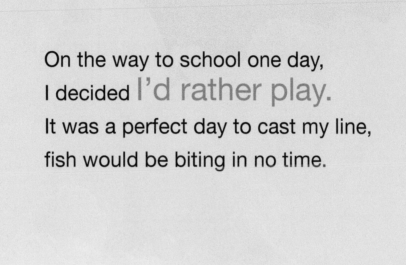

On the way to school one day,
I decided I'd rather play.
It was a perfect day to cast my line,
fish would be biting in no time.

I baited my hook with some old bread,
then dropped my line in and quietly read.
I waited and waited for one little bite,
dreaming of fried fish for dinner that night.

Suddenly my pole dipped and started to shake,
I pulled up my line and caught a snake!
"You're not a fish!" I said to the snake.
"Of course I'm not, for goodness sake!

"My name is Sammy. Let me go!
There are plenty of fish down below."
I put Sammy back in and baited my hook,
threw in my pole and, O, how it shook!

It was a big fish—woahhhhh—I just knew!

I pulled up my pole to find ... an old shoe?

A raggedy old shoe, how could this be?

Where were all the fish in this deep blue sea?

I threw in my pole one last time,
praying a fish would be on the line.
The boat started to rock, and the pole to bend,
this had to be the big one on the other end.

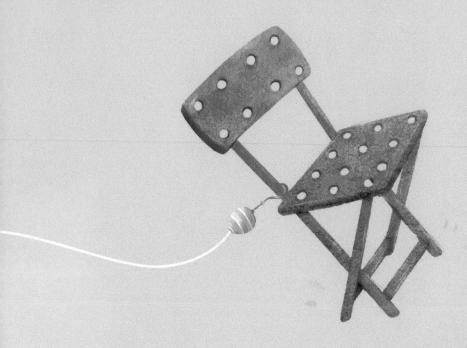

I pulled real hard, straight up in the air,
then out came a rusty old chair.

# "WHERE ARE ALL THE FISH?"

I shouted out loud,
as the sun slipped away behind a cloud.

I looked into the water and what did I see?
A big school of fish, laughing at me!

Right then a big fish jumped into the boat,
wiped off his glasses, and took off his coat.

"I'm Freddy the principal at the School of Fish,
and you, Charles the Croc, are on top of my list!
We will not fall for your bait and hook show,
we are much smarter than you'll ever know.

"That is because we are always in school,
not fishing all day and acting a fool!
Remember what I said the next time you fish."
Then he grabbed his coat and jumped back in—
SPLISH!

I could not believe it, what had I just seen?
A sassy old fish, so bossy and mean.

"He thinks he's so smart, telling me what to do.
I will show you, Mr. Principal, who's smarter than you!"
I cast in my reel one more time,
waiting and watching for a bite on the line.

The sun was setting, I was about to give in,
when something tugged and made the canoe spin.

The boat began to rise, when I saw a big tail,
then I slowly slid down into the mouth of a WHALE!

"HELP! HELP! HELP!" I began to shout.
"I'M BEING EATEN!
PLEASE, GET ME OUT!"
Now I really wished I'd gone to school,
the principal was right, this wasn't so cool.

HELP!
HELP!
HELP!

Freddy and the others heard my plea,
they sprang into action to rescue me.
Freddy dangled a rope down the whale's spout,
"Hang on tight!" he said, as he pulled me right out.

"Looks like I caught *you*, Charles!
Now, who's so bright?"
I hung my head, knowing Freddy was right.

As I crawled upon shore and shook off my scales,
thankful I hadn't become food for a whale,
I waved to the fish, who watched from the sea.
It seemed going to school was the right choice for me.

## About the author: Tracy Detz

Tracy Detz lives on a farm in Wales, Michigan with her eight horses, six cats, two dogs, and her husband, AKA "Tom Cat." She is a therapeutic riding instructor and the owner of Forever Free, Inc., a nonprofit organization for individuals with disabilities that teaches people to overcome obstacles through the way of the marvelous horse. Tracy travels as much as possible and rides like the wind. She loves to read, write, and capture life's precious moments through photography. You can always find her loving on her precious children, people, and animals.

## About the illustrator: Monika Suska

Monika Suska is a children's book illustrator and surface designer who loves, loves, loves her job. Originally from Poland, she moves around a lot; she began illustrating *No Fish for Charles* in Thailand and completed it in Vietnam. Monika loves good food, her husband Tytus, and old Jamaican music, and she is a self-proclaimed "dedicated Trekkie."